Dragons
and other
Beasts

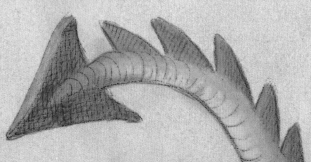

"The Reluctant Dragon" first
appeared in *Dream Days* in 1898.
"The Book of Beasts" first
appeared in *The Book of Dragons* in 1900.

Both books were previously published individually by
Candlewick Press,
2067 Massachusetts Avenue,
Cambridge, MA 02140

The Book of Beasts copyright © 2001 by Inga Moore
The Reluctant Dragon copyright © 2004 by Inga Moore

First edition in this form 2006

This edition published specially for
Barnes & Noble, Inc. 2006 by Candlewick Press

This two-book edition copyright © 2006
by Candlewick Press

Abridgement copyright © 2001, 2004 by Inga Moore
Illustrations copyright © 2001, 2004 by Inga Moore

10 9 8 7 6 5 4 3 2 1

Printed in China

This book has been typeset in
Caslon Five-Forty and Giovanni Book

Barnes & Noble ISBN-13: 978-0-7607-9621-4
Barnes & Noble ISBN-10: 0-7607-9621-1

Candlewick Press ISBN-13: 978-0-7636-3354-7
Candlewick Press ISBN-10: 0-7636-3354-2

visit us at www.candlewick.com

Dragons and other Beasts

ABRIDGED AND ILLUSTRATED BY

Inga Moore

CANDLEWICK PRESS
CAMBRIDGE, MASSACHUSETTS

The Reluctant Dragon

Kenneth Grahame

For Tiggy

Foreword

The Dragon in this story is so wonderfully funny
and friendly (not to mention magnificent!) that
anyone strolling on the Downs on a summer's day
would count themselves very lucky indeed to find
him lolling on the turf in front of his cave.
I myself climbed up to the Downs near Uffington,
in Oxfordshire, hoping to catch a glimpse.
I was one of many visitors to that spot, famous
for the ancient white horse which is etched into
the chalk hillside and for the fight which,
legend has it, took place there between the dragon
and St George. I imagined Kenneth Grahame,
who used to live nearby, coming to this thrilling
place and being inspired to write his delightful tale.
Of course he wrote it a long time ago, but this
heart-warming story of friendship between a
dragon and a boy is as meaningful today
as it has ever been.

Inga Moore

LONG AGO—oh, hundreds of years ago, it was—
in a cottage by the Downs, a shepherd lived with his wife
and their little son. Now, the shepherd spent his days,
and sometimes his nights too, up on the wide, rolling,
windswept Downs, with only the sun and stars and his sheep
for company. But the boy, when he wasn't helping his father,
and often when he was as well, spent much of his time
buried in books that he borrowed from the local gentry.
His parents were very fond of him, and proud of him too.
They knew that book learning came in useful at a pinch,
so they let him read as much as he liked. Natural
history and fairy tales were what he liked mostly.
And he would read them in a mixed-together,
sandwichy sort of way, which is really
rather a sensible way of reading.

One evening the shepherd, who had seemed on edge lately, and not his usual cheerful self, came home all of a tremble, and, sitting down at the table where his wife was sewing, he said:

"It's all up with me, Maria! Never no more can I go up on them Downs!"

"Why, what's the matter?" said his wife. "What can have got you so shook up?"

"You know that cave up there," said the shepherd. "I never liked it, and the sheep never liked it neither, and when sheep don't like a thing, there's generally a reason. Well, there's been noises coming from it lately—sighings and grunts and snoring. So this evening I crept up and had a look—and I saw him!"

"Saw *who*?" asked his wife nervously.

"Why, *him*!" said the shepherd. . . .

"Sticking half out of the cave, he was, as big as four carthorses, and all covered in shiny blue scales. Oh, he was quiet enough, not carrying on or doing anything—I admit that. And yet, *scales*, you know, and claws, and a tail for certain—well, I ain't *used* to 'em, and that's a fact!"

The boy, who had been reading the story of *The Giant with No Heart*, closed his book, yawned, and said:

"Don't worry, Father. It's only a dragon."

"Only a dragon?" cried his father. "What do you mean, *only* a dragon? And how do *you* know so much about it?"

"I just do," replied the boy. "You know about sheep, and weather, and things. *I* know about dragons. I always said that that was a dragon cave. I always said it ought to have a dragon. In fact, I would have been surprised if you'd told me it *hadn't* got a dragon. Now, please, just leave this all to me. I'll stroll up tomorrow evening and have a talk with him."

"He's right, Father," said the sensible mother. "As he says, dragons is *his* line—not ours. It's wonderful him knowing about book beasts. And if by chance that dragon ain't respectable, our boy'll soon find out."

So the next day, after he'd had his tea, the boy strolled up the chalky track that led to the top of the Downs; and there, sure enough, he found the dragon lying in front of his cave. He seemed peaceful enough. Indeed, as the boy drew nearer, he could hear him purring.

"Hello, dragon," he said when he got up to him.

The dragon began to rise politely. But when he saw it was a boy, he frowned and said crossly:

"Now, don't you hit me, or bung stones, or squirt water, or anything. I won't have it, I tell you!"

"Not going to," said the boy. "I've simply looked in to ask how you are. But if I'm in the way, I can easily clear out. Shan't shove myself in where I'm not wanted!"

"No, no," said the dragon hastily, "don't go off in a huff. Fact is, I'm as happy up here as the day's long; always busy, dear fellow, always busy, I assure you! And yet, you know, between ourselves, it *is* a little dull at times."

The boy sat down, bit off a stalk of grass, and chewed it.

"Staying long?" he asked.

"Can't really say yet," replied the dragon. "It seems a nice enough place, and I like the people—what I've seen of 'em—but I've only been here a short time, and one must look about before settling down. Besides—you'd never guess it—but the fact is, I'm *such* a lazy beast!"

"You surprise me," said the boy politely.

"Oh, it's the sad truth," the dragon went on, settling down between his paws, delighted to have found a listener at last, "and I fancy that's really how I came to be still here. You see, the other fellows were always fighting each other and so forth, and chasing knights all over the place—whereas I like to prop my back against a bit of rock and just think."

"What *I* want to know," said the boy, "is what it *is* you like thinking about."

The dragon blushed and looked away. Presently he said:

"Did you ever—just for fun—try to make up poetry?"

"'Course I have," said the boy. "Heaps of it. And some of it's quite good, I feel sure, only there's no one here who cares about it. Mother's very kind, when I read it out to her, and so's Father. But somehow they don't seem to—"

"Exactly," said the dragon. "They don't seem to. Now, you've got culture, you have, I could tell at once, and I should just like to read you a little sonnet I've been working on. I'm awfully pleased to have met you. I hope the other neighbors will be as friendly. There was a nice old gentleman up here last night, but he didn't seem to want to intrude."

"That was my father," said the boy. "I'll introduce you if you like. But, look here, when you talk of neighbors and settling down and so on, I can't help feeling that you haven't actually thought things through. You see, there's no getting over the fact that you're a dragon, and an enemy of the human race."

"Haven't got an enemy in the world!" said the dragon cheerfully. "Too lazy to make 'em, for one thing—"

"Oh, I do wish you would try to understand," said the boy. "When the other people find you, they'll come after you with spears and swords and all sorts of things. The way they look at it, you're a scourge and a pest and a bloodthirsty monster!"

"Not a word of truth in it," said the dragon, wagging his head solemnly. "Why, I wouldn't hurt a fly. Not unless," he added with a wink, "you count boring 'em to death with my poetry! Speaking of which—about this sonnet—"

"Oh, if you *won't* be sensible," said the boy, "I'm going off home. I can't stop for sonnets; my mother's sitting up. I'll look you up tomorrow, and *do* try and realize that you're a pest and a scourge, or you'll find yourself in an awful fix. Good night!"

The boy found it easy enough setting his
parents' minds at rest about his new friend.
Indeed, they took his word without a murmur.
The shepherd was introduced, and while his wife
could not bring herself to actually meet the dragon,
she made no objection to her son spending the evenings
with him quietly, so long as he was home by nine o'clock;
and many a pleasant night they had, sitting on the grass,
while the dragon told stories of old, old times,
when dragons were quite plentiful
and the world was a livelier place
than it is now, and life was full of
thrills and jumps and surprises.

However, the most modest and retiring dragon in the world, if he's as big as four carthorses, is bound to be noticed, and, as the boy had feared, it was soon the talk of the nearby village that a real live dragon sat brooding in the cave on the Downs. Though the villagers were frightened, they were rather proud as well to have a dragon of their own. Still, all were agreed that this sort of thing couldn't go on. The countryside must be freed from this dreadful beast. The fact that not even a hen roost had been harmed since the dragon's arrival wasn't allowed to come into it. He was a dragon and he couldn't deny it. He was a scourge and a pest and he must be gotten rid of. But in spite of much talk, no hero was found willing to take up sword and spear. Meanwhile the dragon lolled on the turf, told antediluvian tales to the boy, and polished up his verses.

One day the boy, walking into the village, found the little street was lined with people chattering, shoving, and ordering each other to stand back.

"What's up?" the boy asked a friend.

"*He's* coming," his friend replied.

"*Who's* coming?"

"Why, St. George, of course. He's coming to slay the dragon! Oh my! Won't there be a jolly fight!"

The boy wriggled his way through to the front of the crowd and waited. Presently there came the sound of cheering and the measured tramp of a great warhorse as St. George paced slowly up the street. The boy's heart beat quicker, and he found himself cheering with the rest, such was the beauty and grace of the hero. His golden armor gleamed, his plumed helmet hung at his side, and his fair hair framed a face gentle beyond telling, till you caught the sternness in his eyes. He drew rein in front of the inn, assuring the villagers that all would be well, that he would free them from their foe. Then he dismounted and went in through the doorway, and the crowd went pouring in after him.

But the boy ran up the hill as fast as he could go.

"He's here, dragon!" he shouted. "You'll have to pull yourself together and *do* something!"

The dragon was busy polishing his scales with a bit of old flannel.

"Don't be *violent*, boy," he said without looking around. "Sit down and get your breath, and then perhaps you'll be good enough to tell me *who's* coming."

"That's right, take it coolly. It's only St. George, that's all," said the boy. "I thought I'd warn you because he's sure to be around early, and he's got the longest, wickedest-looking spear that you ever did see!"

"Well, tell him to go away," said the dragon. "I'm sure he's not nice. Say he can write if he likes. But I won't see him."

"But you've got to," said the boy. "You've got to fight him, you know, because he's St. George and you're the dragon."

"My dear boy," said the dragon. "I've never fought anyone in my life and I'm not going to begin now."

"But he'll cut your head off if you don't," gasped the boy.

"Oh, I think not," said the dragon. "You'll be able to arrange something. You're good at that. Just run down and make it all right—there's a dear chap."

The boy made his way back to the village feeling very down-hearted, for if his dear friend the dragon wouldn't fight, then St. George would surely cut his head off.

"Arrange things indeed!" he muttered gloomily. "Why, the dragon treats the whole thing as if it were an invitation to tea."

As he passed up the little street, the villagers were straggling homeward in high spirits, eagerly discussing the splendid fight that was in store.

St. George now sat alone in the inn, musing on his chances in the fight and the sad tales of robbery and wrongdoing that had been poured into his sympathetic ear.

"May I come in, St. George?" said the boy politely, pausing at the door. "I want to talk to you about the dragon."

"Yes, come in, boy," said the saint kindly. "Another tale of misery and wrong, I fear me. Is it a kind parent, then, of whom the dragon has bereft you? Or some tender sister or brother?"

"Oh, no—nothing of the sort," said the boy. "The fact is, this is a *good* dragon."

"Aha! A good *dragon,*" said St. George, smiling pleasantly. "I quite understand. Believe me, I don't mind in the least that he is no feeble specimen of his loathsome tribe."

"But he *isn't* loathsome," cried the boy. "He's a *good* dragon, and a friend of mine, and he tells me the most beautiful stories you ever heard, all about old times and when he was little. And he's been so kind to Mother; and Mother'd do anything for him. Father likes him too. The fact is, nobody can help liking him, once they *know* him."

"Sit down, and draw your chair up," said St. George. "I like a fellow who sticks up for his friends, and I'm sure the dragon has his good points. However, history teaches us that the most charming of fellows can be the greatest rascals, and all evening I've been listening to tales of murder, theft, and wrong."

"Oh, those villagers," said the boy, "they will tell you any-thing. All they want is a fight. They're the most awful beggars for getting up fights—dogs, bulls, dragons—you name it, so long as it's a fight. And I've no doubt they've been telling you what a hero you are, and how you're bound to win and so on; but let me tell you, I came down the street just now, and they were betting six to four on the dragon!"

"Six to four on the dragon," said St. George sadly, resting his cheek on his hand. "This is an evil world, and I begin to think that not all the wickedness in it is bottled up inside the dragons. But what are we to do? Here we are, the dragon and I, almost face to face, each supposed to be thirsting for the other's blood. I don't see any way out of it."

"I suppose you couldn't be persuaded to go away quietly, could you?" said the boy.

"Impossible, I fear," said the saint. "Quite against the rules. *You* know that."

"Well, then," said the boy. "It's early yet. Would you mind strolling up with me and seeing the dragon and talking it over? It's not far."

"Well, it's irregular," said St. George, "but it seems about the most sensible thing to do."

"I've brought a friend to see you, dragon," said the boy.

The dragon, who had been snoozing in front of his cave as they arrived, woke up with a start.

"This is St. George," said the boy.

"*So* glad to meet you, St. George," said the dragon. "You've been a great traveler, I hear. I've always been rather a stay-at-home. But if you're stopping, I can show you many interesting features of our countryside."

"I think," said St. George, in his frank, pleasant way, "that we ought to get down to business and sort out this little affair of ours. Don't you think that, really, the simplest plan would be to fight it out and let the best man win? They're betting on you, down in the village, you know, but I don't mind."

"But there's nothing to fight about," said the dragon, "and anyhow, I'm not going to, so that settles it!"

"Supposing I make you?" said St. George, rather nettled.

"You can't," said the dragon. "I should only go into my cave and retire for a time. You'd soon get sick of waiting outside, and the moment you'd gone, why, out I'd come again merrily, for I tell you, I like this place and I mean to stay!"

St. George gazed at the fair landscape. "But this would be a beautiful place for a fight," he began again. "These great bare rolling Downs for the arena—and me with my golden armor showing up against your shiny blue scales! Just think what a picture it would make!"

"You can't get at me that way," said the dragon. "It won't work. Not that it wouldn't make a pretty picture as you say," he added, wavering a little.

"You see, dragon," said the boy, "there's got to be a fight of some sort. You can't want to go and stop in that dirty old cave till goodness knows when."

"I suppose," said St. George thoughtfully, "we could always just *pretend* to fight. I must spear you somewhere, of course, but there's such a lot of you that there must be a few *spare* places where it wouldn't hurt. Here, for instance, behind your foreleg. It wouldn't hurt here."

"No, no," said the dragon coyly. "It would tickle—it would make me laugh and that would spoil everything."

"Let's try somewhere else, then," said St. George. "Under your neck, for instance—all these folds of thick skin. If I speared you here, you'd never even know I'd done it!"

"Yes, but are you sure you can hit the right place?" asked the dragon anxiously.

"Of course I am," said St. George. "You leave that to me."

"Look here, dragon," interrupted the boy, "what I want to know is, if there's to be a fight and you're licked, what do *you* get out of it?"

"Tell him, please, St. George," said the dragon. "What *will* happen after I'm vanquished in deadly combat?"

"Well, according to the rules, I shall lead you in triumph down to the marketplace."

"And then?" said the dragon.

"And then there'll be speeches and things," continued St. George. "And I shall explain that you're converted, and so on, and see the error of your ways."

"Yes, yes. Quite so," said the dragon. "And then?"

"Oh, and then," said St. George, "why, and then there'll be the usual banquet, I suppose."

"Exactly," said the dragon, "and that's where *I* come in. I'm going into society, I am. Once people see the likable sort of fellow I really am, why, I shall be invited everywhere. So now that's all settled, and if you don't mind—don't want to turn you out, but . . ."

"Remember, you'll have to do your proper share of the fighting, dragon!" said St. George, as he took the hint and turned to go. "I mean ramping, and breathing fire, and so on!"

"It's surprising how one gets out of practice," said the dragon, "but I'll do my best. Good night!"

The next morning, people began streaming up to the Downs at an early hour, in their Sunday clothes and carrying baskets with bottlenecks sticking out of them. Places were chosen and the higher ground was soon thick with sightseers.

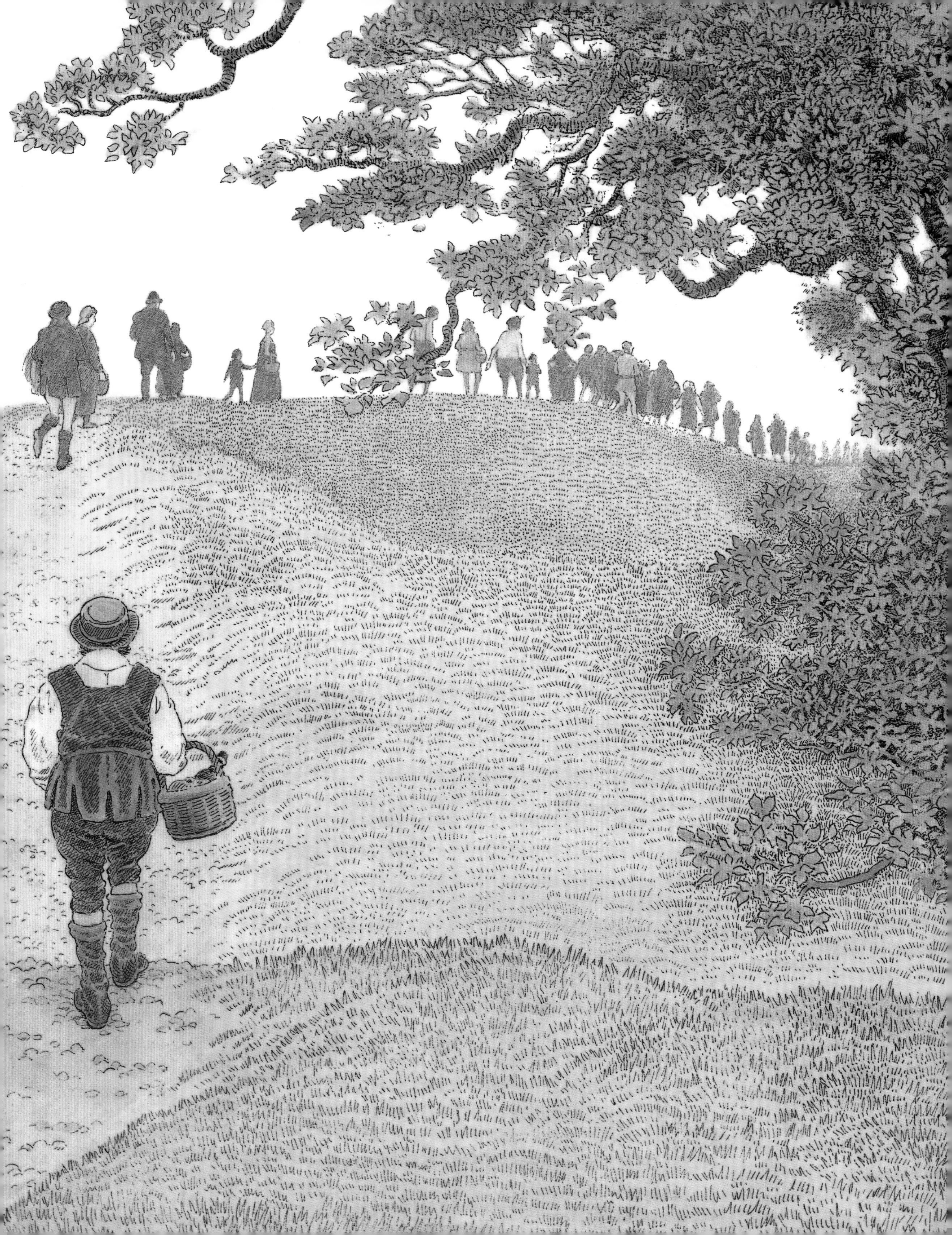

The boy found himself a good place, well up toward the cave. He was feeling anxious. Could the dragon be depended upon? He might be too nervous to show up. There was no sign of him in the cave. Could he have done a moonlight flit?

Presently the sound of cheering
told him something was happening.
A minute more and St. George's red plumes
topped the hill. The saint rode slowly forth
on his tall warhorse, his great spear held erect,
the little pennon, crimson-crossed, fluttering at its point.
He drew rein and waited.

The crowd leaned forward expectantly.

"Now then, dragon!" hissed the boy. And the dragon, who,
it turned out, had liked the idea of play-acting immensely,
and who had been up since dawn rehearsing his part,
was not about to let him down.

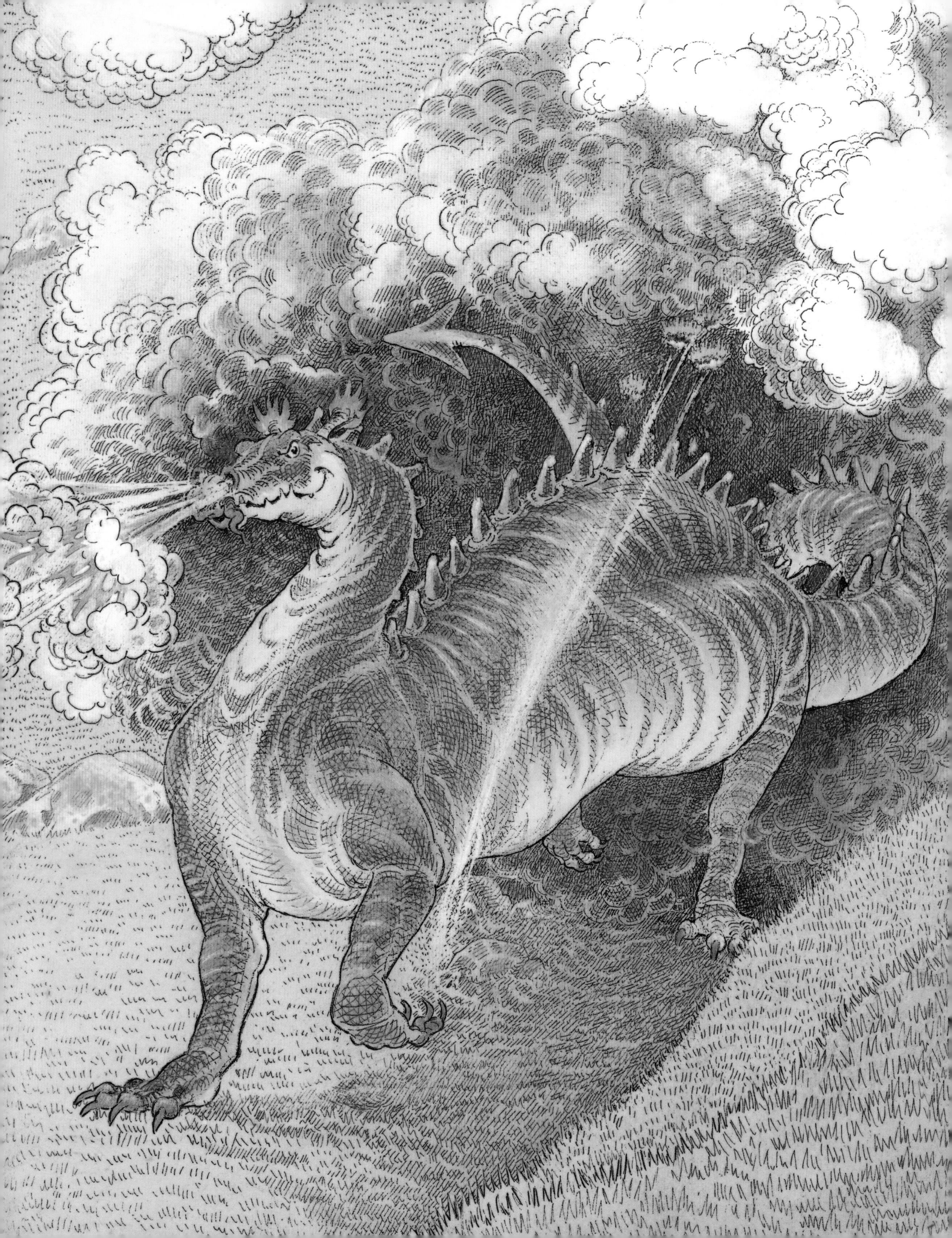

A low rumble, mingled with snorts, was heard;
it rose to a bellowing roar that seemed to fill the air.
Clouds of smoke billowed from the mouth of the cave,
and then the dragon himself, shining, sea blue, magnificent,
pranced splendidly forth, and everybody said, "Oo-oo-oo!"
His scales were glittering, his long spiky tail lashed his sides,
and his claws tore up the turf and sent it flying high over
his back, and smoke and fire jetted from his nostrils.

"Oh, well done, dragon!" cried the boy.

St. George lowered his spear, bent his head, dug his heels
into his horse's sides, and came thundering over the turf.
The dragon charged with a roar and a squeal—
a great blue whirling combination of scales
and snorts and clashing jaws and spikes.

"Missed!" yelled the crowd. There was a muddle
of golden armor and blue scales and a spiky tail,
and then the great horse, tearing at his bit,
carried the saint, his spear swinging,
almost to the mouth of the cave.

The dragon sat down and barked viciously,
while St. George, with difficulty, pulled his
horse around into position.
  End of round one, thought the boy.
How well they both pulled it off,
and what a good play-actor
the dragon is!

At last St. George managed to get his horse to stand steady, and, looking around as he wiped his brow, he caught sight of the boy and smiled and nodded.

The dragon, meanwhile, was using the interval to give a ramping performance in front of the crowd. Ramping, it should be explained, consists of running around and around in a wide circle, sending waves and ripples of movement along the whole length of your spine, from your ears right down to the spike at the end of your tail.

"Time!" yelled everybody. The dragon left off his ramping and began to leap from one side to the other with huge bounds. This naturally upset the horse, who swerved violently. The saint only just saved himself, and as they shot past, the dragon snapped viciously at the horse's tail, which sent the poor beast careering madly over the Downs, so that the language of the saint, who had lost a stirrup, could fortunately not be heard.

In round two, the crowd was clearly warming to the dragon. They liked a fellow who could hold his own so well; and many encouraging remarks reached the ears of our friend as he went strutting to and fro, his chest thrust out and his tail in the air, hugely enjoying his new popularity.

St. George had dismounted and was tightening his girths and telling his horse exactly what he thought of him. So the boy made his way down to the saint's end and held his spear for him.

"It's been a jolly fight, St. George!" he said. "Will it last much longer?"

"I think not," replied the saint. "The fact is, your silly friend's getting conceited, now they've begun cheering him. He'll soon start playing the fool, and there's no telling where it will stop. I'd better get it over with this round."

He swung into his saddle and took his spear from the boy. "Now, don't you worry," he said. "I've marked the spot exactly."

St. George shortened his spear, bringing the butt well up under his arm; and, instead of galloping as before, he trotted smartly up to the dragon, who crouched, flicking his tail till it cracked like a great cart whip. The saint wheeled and circled around his opponent, keeping his eye on the spare place, while the dragon paced slowly and very warily beside the saint, feinting from time to time with his head. So the two sparred for an opening, while the crowd held their breath.

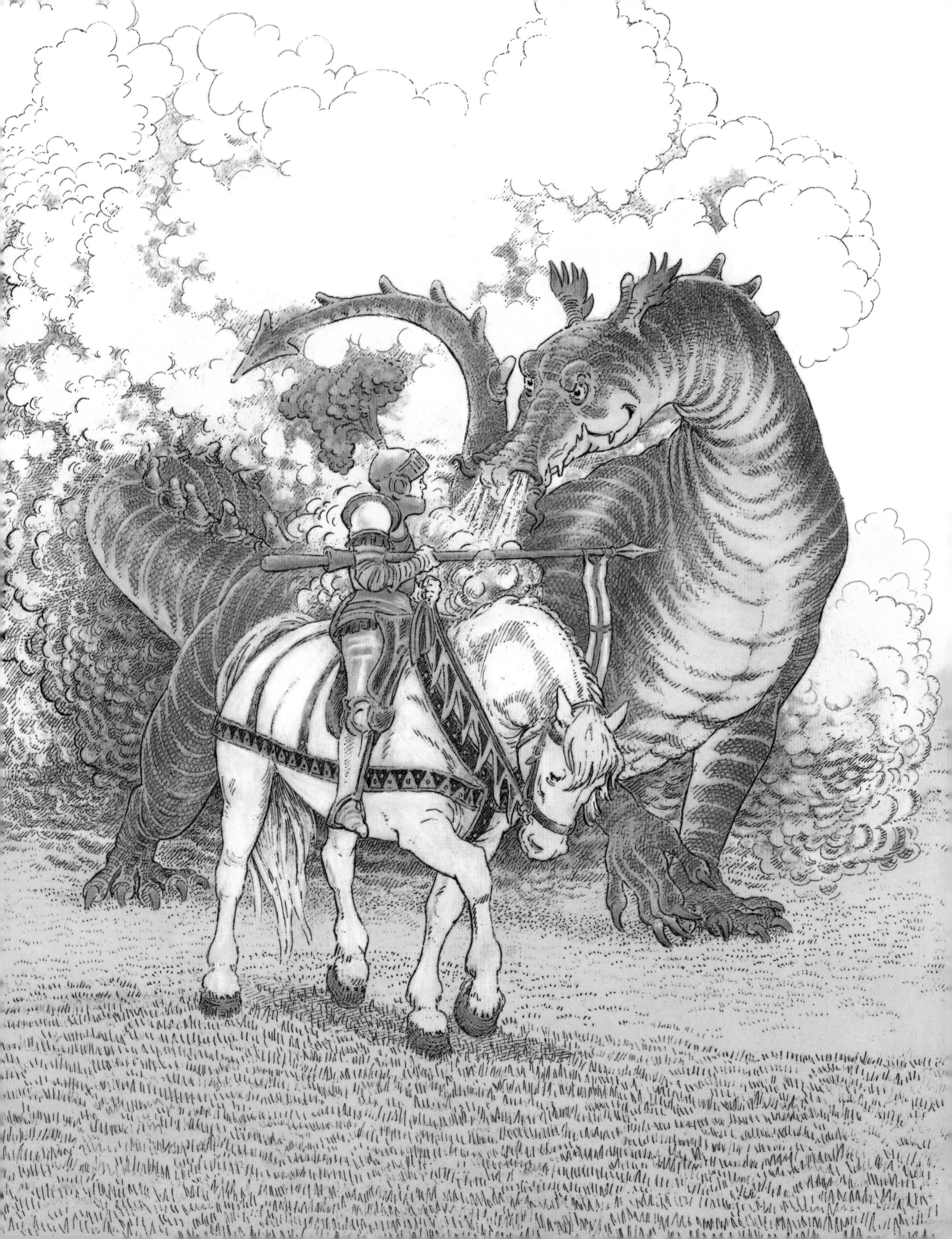

Though the round lasted for some minutes, the end was so swift that all the boy saw was a lightning movement of the saint's arm and then a whirl of spikes and claws and flying bits of turf. The dust cleared, the crowd whooped and ran in cheering, and the boy saw that the dragon was down, pinned to the earth by the spear.

It all seemed so real that the boy ran in breathlessly, hoping the dear old dragon wasn't really hurt. But as he drew near, the dragon lifted one eyelid and winked solemnly. He was held fast to the earth by the neck, but the saint had hit the spare place agreed upon, and it didn't even seem to tickle.

"Bain't you goin' to cut 'is 'ead orf, mister?"
asked one of the crowd. He had backed the dragon,
and naturally felt a little sore.
     "There's no hurry," replied St. George.
"I think we'll go down to the village first,
     and have some refreshment, and then
          I'll give him a good talking-to,
               and you'll find he'll be
                    a very different dragon!"

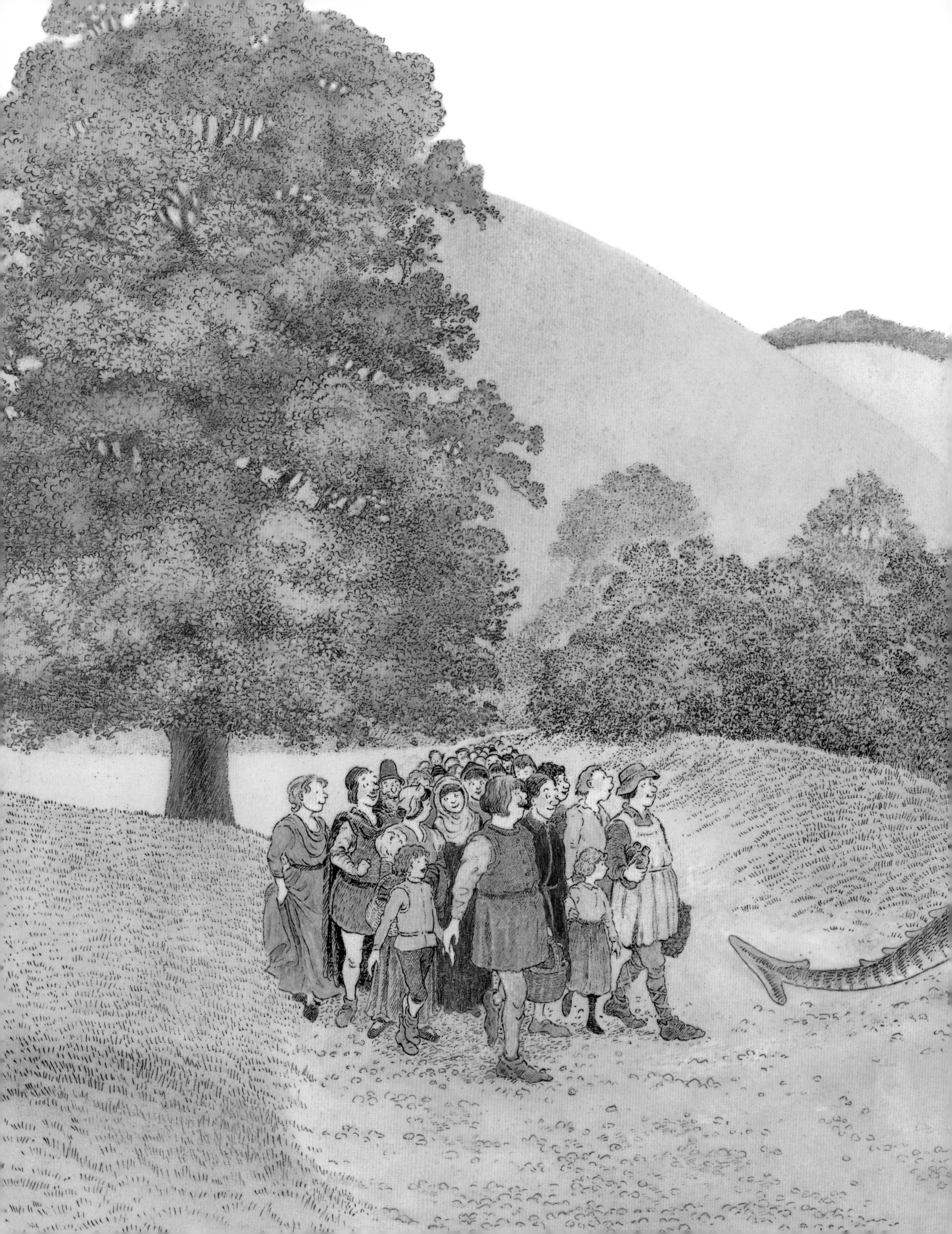

At that magic word *refreshment*, the whole crowd formed up
in a procession and waited for the signal to start. St. George,
hauling on his spear, released the dragon, who rose and shook
himself and ran his eye over his spikes and scales and things,
to see that they were all in order. Then the saint mounted
and led everybody back to the village, with the dragon
following meekly in the company of the boy, while
the thirsty crowd kept respectfully behind.

After refreshments, St. George made a speech, in which he told the villagers that he had freed them from their direful foe, and at a great deal of trouble and inconvenience to himself. So now they weren't to go about grumbling and pretending they'd got grievances, because they hadn't. And they should not be so fond of fights, because next time they might have to do the fighting themselves, which wouldn't be the same thing at all. Then he told them that the dragon had been thinking it over and saw that there were two sides to every question, and he wasn't going to do it anymore, and if they were good, perhaps he'd stay and settle down. So they must make friends, and not be prejudiced and go about thinking that they knew everything, because they didn't, not by a long way. And he warned them about the sin of making up gossip and thinking other people would believe them. Then there was much repentant cheering. And then everyone went off to get ready for the banquet.

Banquets are always pleasant things, consisting mostly, as they do, of eating and drinking; but the especially nice thing about a banquet is that it comes when something's over, and there's nothing more to worry about, and tomorrow seems a long way off. St. George was happy because there had been a fight and he hadn't had to kill anyone; he didn't really like killing, though he often had to do it. The dragon was happy because there had been a fight, and far from being hurt in it, he had won popularity and a sure footing in society. The boy was happy because there had been a fight, and in spite of it all, his two friends were on the best of terms.

And all the others were happy because there had been a fight, and—well, they didn't need any other reason. The dragon took great pains to say the right thing to everybody and proved to be the life and soul of the party; while the saint and the boy, looking on, felt as if they were merely guests at a feast held entirely in honor of the dragon. But they didn't mind, being good fellows, and the dragon was not in the least bit forgetful. On the contrary, every so often he leaned over toward the boy and said, "Look here! You will see me home afterward, won't you?" And the boy always nodded, though he had promised his mother not to be out late.

At last the banquet was over. The guests had dropped away with many good-nights and invitations, and the dragon, who had seen the last of them off, went out into the street, followed by the boy. The dragon sighed, sat down, and gazed at the stars.

"Jolly night it's been!" he said. "Jolly stars! Jolly little place this! Think I'll just sit here for a bit. Don't feel like climbing up that hill just yet."

St. George, who was outside strolling in the cool night air, saw them sitting there—the great dragon and the little boy.

"Now, look here, dragon," said the saint firmly. "This little fellow is waiting to see you home, and you *know* he ought to be in bed by now, and what his mother'll say I *don't* know."

"And so he *shall* go to bed!" cried the dragon, getting up. "Poor little chap. Fancy him being up at this hour! Why, it's a shame, that's what it is! But come along, let's have no more of this shilly-shallying. Off we go—that's the way."

So they set off up the hill,
the saint, the dragon, and the boy.
The lights in the little village began to
go out, but there were stars and a late moon, as
they climbed to the Downs together.

And, as they turned the last corner and disappeared from view, snatches of an old song were borne back on the night breeze. I can't be certain which of them was singing, but I *think* it was the dragon!

The
Book of
Beasts

E. Nesbit

For Creakles, my very own Hippogriff

Foreword

The Book of Beasts was first published
in 1900 in a collection of stories written by
Edith Nesbit called *The Book of Dragons.*
I was delighted to have the opportunity,
one hundred years later, to bring to life
once more the fearsome Red Dragon,
and our heroes, Lionel and the beautiful
Hippogriff, which incidentally is not
the Hippogriff of tradition.

Not for a moment has it been a task.
Quite the contrary, it has been fun from
start to finish. For this picture book edition,
I have made with great care and respect an
abridgement of the text which was written,
I feel sure we would all agree, by one of
the finest children's writers of all time.

Inga Moore

LIONEL HAPPENED to be building a Palace when the news came. There was a knock at the door and voices talking downstairs and then, quite suddenly, Nurse came in and said:

Master Lionel, dear, they've come to fetch you to go and be King.

In the drawing room there were two very grave-looking gentlemen in red robes with fur, and gold coronets with velvet sticking up out of the middle like cream in jam tarts.

They bowed low to Lionel and said:

Sire, your great-great-great-great-great-grandfather has died . . .

and now you have got to come and be King.

And they led the way to a coach with eight white horses, which was drawn up in front of the house where Lionel lived. It was No. 7, on the left-hand side of the street as you go up.

So off went Lionel to be made a King. He had never expected to be a King any more than you have. All the bells of the churches were ringing like mad, and people were shouting;

Long live Lionel!

"I thought we were a Republic," said Lionel. "I'm sure there hasn't been a King for some time."

The grave gentlemen, who were the Chancellor and the Prime Minister, explained:

"Since your great-great-great-great-great-grandfather's death, your loyal people have been saving up to buy you a crown—so much a week, you know, according to people's means—sixpence a week from those who have first-rate pocket money, down to a halfpenny a week from those who haven't."

"But didn't my great-great-however-much-it-is-grandfather have a crown?"

"Yes, but he sold it to buy books. A very good King he was—but he was fond of books."

Just then the carriage stopped and Lionel was taken out to be crowned. Being crowned is more tiring than you would suppose, and by the time it was over, and Lionel had worn the Royal robes for an hour or two and had had his hand kissed by everybody, he was quite worn out, and was very glad to get into the Palace nursery.

Nurse was there and tea was ready,
and after tea Lionel said:
"I think I should like a book."
So he went down to the library,
and when Lionel came in,
the Prime Minister and the
Chancellor bowed very low,
and Lionel cried:

Oh, what a worldful of books! Are they yours?

"They are yours, your Majesty," answered the Chancellor. "They were the property of your great-great —"

"Well," Lionel interrupted, "I shall read them all. I love to read. I am so glad I learned to read."

"If I might advise your Majesty," said the Prime Minister. "I should *not* read these books. Your great —"

"Yes?" said Lionel quickly.

"He was a little — well, strange."

"Mad?" asked Lionel cheerfully.

"No, no," — both gentlemen were shocked. "Not mad. The fact is, your great —"

"Go on," said Lionel.

"Was *called* a wizard."

"But he wasn't?"

"Of course not. But I wouldn't touch his books."

"Just this one," cried Lionel, laying his hands on a great brown book that lay on the table. It had gold patterns on the leather and gold clasps with turquoises and rubies in the twists. "I *must* look at this one."

For on the back in big letters he read: *The Book of Beasts.*

The Chancellor said, "Don't be a silly little King." But Lionel had got the gold clasps undone, and he opened the first page, and there was a Butterfly, all red, and brown, and yellow, and blue, so beautifully painted that it looked as if it were alive.

"There," said Lionel, "isn't that lovely?" But as he spoke, the Butterfly fluttered its wings on the old yellow page and flew up and out of the window.

"Well!" said the Prime Minister. "That's magic, that is."

But the King had turned the next page and there was a shining blue bird. Under him was written, "Blue Bird of Paradise." The Blue Bird fluttered his wings on the old yellow page and spread them and flew out of the book.

Then the Prime Minister snatched the book
away from the King and shut it, and put it on
a very high shelf. And the Chancellor said:
"You're a naughty, disobedient little King,"
and was very angry indeed.

"I don't see that I've done any harm," said Lionel.

"No harm?" said the Chancellor. "Ah, but how do you
know what might have been on the next page—
a snake or a centipede or a revolutionist,
or something like that."

"Well, I'm sorry," said Lionel. "Come,
let's kiss and be friends."

So he kissed the Prime Minister
and they settled down for a quiet
game of noughts and crosses,
while the Chancellor went to
add up his accounts.

But when Lionel was in bed he could not sleep for thinking of the book, and when the moon was shining with all her might, he crept down to the library and climbed up and got *The Book of Beasts*. He opened it, and saw the empty pages with "Butterfly" and "Blue Bird of Paradise" underneath. Then he turned the next page. There was some sort of red thing sitting under a palm tree, and under it was written "Dragon." The Dragon did not move, and the King shut the book rather quickly and went back to bed.

But the next day he wanted another look,
so he got the book out into the garden,
and when he undid the clasps, the book
opened all by itself at the picture with
"Dragon" underneath, and the sun fell full
upon the page. And then, quite suddenly,
a great Red Dragon came out of the book
and spread vast scarlet wings and flew away
across the garden to the hills, and Lionel
was left with the empty page before him—
empty except for the green palm tree and
the yellow desert, and the little streaks
of red where the paint brush had
gone outside the pencil outline
of the Red Dragon.

Lionel began to cry. He had not been King twenty-four hours, and already he had let loose a Dragon to worry his faithful subjects. And they had been saving up so long to buy him a crown and everything.

Then the Chancellor and the Prime Minister and the Nurse all came running to see what the matter was.

Lionel, in floods of tears, said:

It's a Red Dragon, and it's flown away to the hills.

And when the Chancellor and the Prime
Minister saw the book, they said:

*You
naughty little
King!*

*Put
him to bed,
Nurse!*

And they hurried
off to consult the police
to see what could be done.
Everyone did what they could.
They sat on committees and
stood on guard. They lay
in wait for the Dragon
but he stayed up in
the hills.

Then on Saturday, in the afternoon, the Dragon suddenly swooped down on the common in all his hideous redness and carried off the Football Players, umpires, goalposts, football, and all.

On the following Saturday he ate the Parliament, and an Orphanage on the Saturday after that.

Lionel was very, very unhappy. He felt that it was his duty to do something. The question was, what?

The Blue Bird that had come out of the book used to sing nicely in the Palace rose garden, and the Butterfly was very tame. So Lionel saw that *all* the creatures in *The Book of Beasts* could not be wicked, like the Dragon, and he thought:

"Suppose I could get another beast out who would fight the Dragon?"

So he took *The Book of Beasts* out into the rose garden and opened the page next to the one where the Dragon had been just a tiny bit to see what the name was. He could only see "cora," but he felt the middle of the page swelling up thick with the creature that was trying to come out, and it was only by putting the book down and sitting on it suddenly, very hard, that he managed to get it shut. Then he fastened the clasps and sent for the Chancellor, who had been ill on Saturday week, and

so had not been eaten with the rest
of the Parliament,
and he said:

What animal ends in "cora"?

The Manticora, of course.

"What is he like?" asked the King.

"He is the sworn foe of Dragons," said the Chancellor.
"He drinks their blood. He is yellow, with the body of
a lion and the face of a man. I wish we had a Manticora
here now. But the last one died years ago — worse luck!"

Then the King ran and opened the book at the page that had "cora" on it, and there was the Manticora, just as the Chancellor had described.

And in a few minutes the Manticora came sleepily out of the book, rubbing his eyes and mewing piteously.

And when Lionel said:

Go and fight the Dragon!

he put his tail between his legs
and ran away. He went and hid behind the
Town Hall, and at night, when the people were asleep,
he went around and ate all the pussycats in the town.
And then he mewed more than ever.

On Saturday morning the Dragon came looking for the Manticora, who was not at all the Dragon-fighting kind, and found him trying to hide himself in the Post Office among the ten o'clock mail. The Dragon fell on the Manticora at once, and the mewings were heard all over town. Then there was a sad silence, and presently the Dragon came walking down the Post Office steps spitting fire and smoke, and tufts of Manticora fur.

The Dragon was a nuisance for the whole of Saturday, except during the hour of noon, and then he had to rest under a tree or he would have caught fire from the heat of the sun. You see, he was very hot to begin with.

At last came a Saturday when the King said:

*Nurse, dear, kiss me in case I never come back, but I **must** try to save the people.*

"Well, if you must, you must," said Nurse, "but don't tear your clothes or get your feet wet."

So off he went.

The Blue Bird sang more sweetly than ever, and the Butterfly shone brightly, as Lionel once more carried *The Book of Beasts* out into the rose garden, and opened it—very quickly, so that he might not change his mind. The book fell open almost in the middle and there was written at the bottom of the page, "Hippogriff," and before Lionel had time to see what the picture was, there was a fluttering of wings and a stamping of hoofs, and a soft, friendly neighing; and there came out of the book a beautiful white horse with a long, long, white mane and a long, long, white tail, and he had great wings like swans' wings, and the kindest eyes in the world, and he stood there among the roses.

The Hippogriff rubbed his silky-soft, milky-white nose against the little King's shoulder. And the Blue Bird's song was very loud and sweet.

Then suddenly the King saw coming through the sky the great wicked shape of the Red Dragon. And he knew at once what he must do. He caught up *The Book of Beasts* and jumped on the back of the gentle, beautiful Hippogriff, and leaning down he whispered in the sharp white ear:

Fly, dear Hippogriff, fly your very fastest to the Pebbly Waste.

And when the Dragon saw them start,
he turned and flew after them,
with his great wings flapping
like clouds at sunset.

But the Dragon could not catch the Hippogriff.

The red wings were bigger than the white ones,

but they were not so strong, and the white-winged horse

flew away, away, and away, with the Dragon pursuing,

till he reached the very middle of the Pebbly Waste.

Now, the Pebbly Waste is like parts of the seaside—all round, loose, shifting stones, and there is no grass there and no tree within a hundred miles of it.

Lionel jumped off the white horse's back in the middle of the Pebbly Waste, and he unclasped *The Book of Beasts* and laid it open on the pebbles. He had just jumped back onto his horse when up came the Dragon.

He was flying very feebly, and looking around everywhere for a tree, for it was just on the stroke of twelve, the sun was shining like a gold guinea in the blue sky, and there was not a tree for a hundred miles.

The white-winged horse flew round and round
the Dragon as he writhed on the pebbles.
He was getting very hot: indeed, parts of him
had begun to smoke. He knew he must certainly
catch fire unless he could get under a tree. He made
a snatch with his red claws at the King and Hippogriff,
but he was too feeble to reach them, and besides,
he did not dare to over-exert himself
for fear he should get any hotter.

It was then he saw *The Book
of Beasts* lying on the pebbles,
open at the page with
"Dragon" written
at the bottom.

He looked, and he looked again, and then,
with one last squirm of rage, the Dragon
wriggled himself back into the picture,
and sat down under the palm tree,
and the page was a little singed
as he went in.

As soon as Lionel saw the Dragon had been forced to go and sit under his own palm tree because it was the only tree there, he jumped off his horse, shut the book with a BANG! and cried:

HURRAH!

And he clasped the book very tight with the turquoise and ruby clasps.

"Oh, my dear Hippogriff," he cried, "you are the bravest, most beautiful—"

"Hush!" whispered the Hippogriff, modestly. "Don't you see we are not alone?"

And indeed there was quite a crowd around them on the Pebbly Waste: the Prime Minister and the Parliament and the Football Players, the Orphanage and the Manticora, indeed everyone who had been eaten by the Dragon.

You see, it was a tight fit even for a Dragon inside the book—so, of course, he had to leave them outside.

They all got home somehow, and all lived happy
ever after.

When the King asked the Manticora where he would like
to live, he begged to be allowed to go back into the book.
"I do not care for public life," he said.

Of course he knew his way back onto his own page,
so there was no danger of letting out the Dragon.
And of course he left the pussycats outside,
because there was no room
for them in the book.

As for the beautiful,
white-winged Hippogriff,
he accepted the position of
the King's Own Hippogriff.

And the Blue Bird and Butterfly
sing and flutter among the lilies
and roses of the Palace garden
to this very day.

About the Author

Kenneth Grahame was born in Scotland in 1859. From the age of five he lived with his grandmother in Cookham Dean, Berkshire, where he spent a lot of time on the banks of the River Thames. Later in his life he lived in Blewberry by the Berkshire Downs. It was here that he wrote "The Reluctant Dragon," which was first published in *Dream Days* in 1898, ten years before the publication of his most famous work, *The Wind in the Willows* (1908).

THE BOOK OF BEASTS

About the Author

Edith Nesbit (1858–1924) spent her childhood in France and Germany and later lived in England. She began writing stories of fantasy and adventure for children in the early 1890s and soon set herself apart from other such authors of the time because of her contemporary settings and very real, strong-willed young characters. E. Nesbit's novels include *The Story of the Treasure Seekers* (1899), *Five Children and It* (1902), *The Phoenix and the Carpet* (1904), and *The Railway Children* (1906).

About the Illustrator

Inga Moore has written and illustrated many picture books for children. *School Library Journal* gave her abridged version of *The Reluctant Dragon* a starred review and said of her work: "The colored-pencil and ink illustrations demonstrate her gift for capturing the atmosphere of a story." Moore received similar acclaim for *The Book of Beasts* from *Newsday,* whose reviewer noted: "The picture of the dragon rising up out of the little king's book and beyond the edges of the page in our hands makes my three-year-old gasp every time."